MAURICE'S ROOM

MAURICE'S ROOM

BY
PAULA FOX

PICTURES BY
INGRID FETZ

MACMILLAN PUBLISHING COMPANY
NEW YORK

Macmillan Publishing Company
866 Third Avenue, New York, N.Y. 10022
Collier Macmillan Canada, Inc.

First published 1966; reissued 1985.
Printed in the United States of America
10 9 8 7 6 5 4 3 2

Library of Congress Cataloging in Publication Data
Fox, Paula.
Maurice's room.
First published in 1966.
Summary: Eight-year-old Maurice's struggle to
protect his bedroom full of treasured "junk" from
unsympathetic parents undergoes a transformation
when the family moves to the country.
1. Children's stories, American. [1. Bedrooms—
Fiction. 2. Family life—Fiction. 3. City and town
life—Fiction] I. Fetz, Ingrid, ill. II. Title.
PZ7.F838Mau   1985   [Fic]   85-7200
ISBN 0-02-735490-3

FOR GABE

CONTENTS

THE COLLECTION

Maurice's room measured six long steps in one direction and five in the other. The distance from the floor to the ceiling was three times higher than Maurice. There was one window through which Maurice could see several other windows as well as a piece of the sky. From the middle of the ceiling dangled a long string, the kind used to tie up packages of laundry. Attached to the end of the string was a dried octopus. It was the newest addition to Maurice's collection. When his mother or father walked into his room—which wasn't often—the octopus swung back and forth a little in the draught.

8

Maurice had used a ladder to climb up high enough to tack the string to the ceiling. The ladder was still leaning against the wall. Instead of returning it to Mr. Klenk, the janitor of his building, from whom he had borrowed it, Maurice was using the steps for shelves. Even though Maurice's father, Mr. Henry, had put up a dozen shelves around the room for all of Maurice's things, there still weren't enough.

Maurice knew how to walk around his room without stepping on anything, and so did his friend Jacob. But no one else did.

As his mother and father often said to visitors, it was astonishing how much junk a person could find in one city block. His mother said Maurice kept their block clean because he brought up everything from the street to his room. His father said Maurice ought to get a salary from the Department of Sanitation because of all the work he was doing in cleaning up the city. At least once a month Mr. and Mrs. Henry talked about moving to the country. It would be better for Maurice, they said. But then they would decide to wait a little longer.

Some visitors said that collections like Maurice's showed that a child would become a great scientist. Many great scientists had collected junk when they were eight years old. Other visitors said Maurice would outgrow his collection and become interested in other things, such as money or armies. Some suggested to the Henrys that they ought to buy Maurice a dog, or send him to music school so that his time might be spent more usefully.

In his room Maurice had a bottle full of dead beetles, a powdery drift of white moths in a cup without a handle, a squirrel hide tacked to a board, a snakeskin on a wire hanger, a raccoon tail, a glass of shrimp eggs, a plate of mealy worms, a box of turtle food.

There were things with which to make other things, such as nails of different sizes, screws, wire, butterfly bolts, scraps of wood, sockets, filaments from electric-light bulbs, cardboard from grocery boxes, two orange crates, a handsaw and a hammer. On the top of a chest of drawers Maurice kept stones and pebbles, dried tar balls, fragments of brick, pieces of colored bottle glass that had been worn smooth, and gray rocks that glistened with mica.

On his window sill there was a heap of dried moss next to a turtle bowl in which several salamanders lived half hidden by mud and wet grass. On the same sill he kept some plants from the five-and-ten-

cent store. They looked dead. Now and then a cactus would put out a new shoot.

In another bowl on a table covered with yellow oilcloth were four painted turtles that were getting quite soft in the shell, and in a corner, in a square fish bowl with a chicken-wire roof, lived a garter snake and a lizard. An old hamster in his cage slept or filled his pouches with dried carrots or ran on his wheel. The wheel, which needed an oiling, screeched all night, the time the hamster preferred for exercise. But the noise didn't keep Maurice awake, only his parents. In a pickle jar, a garden spider sat in a forked twig, her egg sack just below her. Maurice also had a bird. It was a robin, blind in one eye and unable to find food for itself.

On the floor were coffee cans with things in them; an eggbeater with a missing gear, a pile of dead starfish, cigar boxes, clockworks, hinges, and a very large grater with sharp dents on all four of its sides. The grater was orange with rust, and it stood in the middle of the room beneath the octopus. You would have to use a magnifying glass to see all the other things Maurice had found.

His bed had two blankets and a pillow without a pillowcase. Sometimes a small goose feather pricked its way through the ticking, and Maurice would put it away in an envelope. He had used two pillowcases for his collecting expeditions, and after that his mother wouldn't give him any more.

There was one tidy corner in Maurice's room. It was where he had pushed his Christmas toys. They were a month old now, and the dust covered them evenly. They were like furniture or bathroom fixtures. Maurice felt there wasn't much to be done with them.

It was the end of January, and Maurice had just come home from school. He put his books on his bed and went to see what the snake was doing. It was lying on its rock. The lizard was watching it. The robin was so still it looked stuffed. But it cocked its head when Maurice whistled at it. The hamster was hiding bits of carrot in the sawdust at the bottom of its cage. The salamanders had buried themselves in the mud. Maurice was arranging little piles of food for his animals when he heard his uncle's voice from down the hall.

"Lily," his uncle was saying t
ought to dynamite that room!"

"There must be another way

"You'd better give it up," said
will never clean it."

"If we lived in the country,
would be different," said
his mother.

"Perhaps," said his uncle.
Maurice took two walnuts
from his pocket and cracked
them together. His mother came
to the door.

"Get everything off the floor,"
she said in a low, even voice as
though she were counting moving freight cars.

"Where will I put things?"
asked Maurice.

"I don't care," she said. "But
clear the floor! Or else I'll bring
in the broom, the dustpan, and
a very large box. And that will
be that!"

The doorbell rang. It was Jacob.

"Jacob can help you," his mother said.
Jacob was seven, but he looked bigger than

Maurice. It was because he was wearing so many clothes—scarves, mittens, sweaters, two hats, and several pairs of socks. He began to take off his outer clothing, laying each item in a pile at his feet. Meanwhile Maurice explained the predicament.

"What are we going to do?" asked Jacob.

Maurice looked at the chest of drawers. The pebbles and rocks had been moved to the floor, and the chest was now covered with oatmeal boxes. He looked at the table. He could barely see the yellow oilcloth because it was hidden by sections of a witch doctor's mask he and Jacob had begun to make the week before. The turtles had been moved next to the salamanders on the window sill.

"There are five more floors in this room if you count the walls and ceiling," Maurice said to Jacob. Jacob looked smaller and thinner now that he was down to his shirt and pants.

"I see," said Jacob.

"We'll have to ask Mr. Klenk to help us," said Maurice.

Jacob began to sort out nails. Then he stopped. "But we won't be able to do that with everything! And how can we get it all done in just a day?"

"Mr. Klenk will know," said Maurice.

3.   THE JANITOR

Mr. Klenk, the janitor, lived in the basement five floors down. The basement smelled like wet mops, damp cement, pipes, and old furniture stuffing. But it was clean. Mr. Klenk had told Maurice that he couldn't relax a second or he would be drowned by the rubbish that poured out of all the apartments. "Overwhelming!" Mr. Klenk often exclaimed.

"It's a race between me and the junk," he would say. "If I let it get an edge on me, I'll get shoved right out of the city." But Mr. Klenk didn't seem to feel the same way about Maurice's collection.

"Well, you're selective, my boy," he had said once, giving Maurice a caramel. "Besides, I suspect you've got something in mind for all that stuff of yours."

The two boys rang the janitor's bell. Mr. Klenk opened his door, blowing out a cloud of cigar smoke.

"I have to get everything off the floor," Maurice said. "Could you help us a little?"

"What do you have in mind?"

"There's plenty of space on the walls," said Maurice.

Mr. Klenk nodded and puffed on his cigar. "I know," he said. "But you didn't bring back my ladder, did you?"

"He forgot," said Jacob timidly. Mr. Klenk peered through the cigar smoke. Jacob backed away. The janitor in the building where Jacob lived sat in a big collapsed steamer trunk all day just waiting, Jacob was sure, for boys to wander by so he could pounce on them.

"Can you come now?" asked Maurice.

"Let's go," answered Mr. Klenk.

When they reached Maurice's room, Mr. Klenk stopped at the doorway.

"How am I supposed to get in there?" he asked.

Jacob cleared a path for him. Maurice took all the things off the ladder steps, and in a few minutes Mr. Klenk was at work.

First Maurice chose the starfish. He handed it to Jacob, who held it up to Mr. Klenk on the ladder. Next came the rusty grater. In an hour everything was hanging either from the ceiling or from the walls. The animals paid no attention to the fact that they were suspended above the floor. The hamster went to sleep; his cage swung gently like a hammock in a light breeze.

By six o'clock, the floor boards appeared. It was a good floor, and Maurice and Jacob sat down on it.

"Now we have room for more things," said Maurice.

Maurice's mother and his uncle came to the door.

"Wow!" said Uncle.

Mrs. Henry looked pale. "I didn't have *that* in mind," she said.

"Well, Lily, they've cleared the floor," said the uncle. He looked at Maurice. "I have a surprise," he said. "I'm going to bring Patsy here to spend a week with you."

Then his uncle winked at Mrs. Henry. "You'll see," he said to her. "Patsy will take his mind off all of this." Maurice's mother looked doubtful.

"Who is Patsy?" asked Jacob.

"Who is Patsy!" repeated the uncle, as though astonished. "Tell him, Maurice."

"A dog," said Maurice. "A dumb fat dog," he added in a whisper to Jacob.

After Maurice's uncle and Mrs. Henry went back to the kitchen, Mr. Klenk picked up his ladder and started to leave. Then he seemed to remember something. He tapped Maurice on the shoulder.

"Would you like a stuffed bear?" he asked.

"I'd like a bear," Maurice said.

"A tenant left it when he moved out," said Mr. Klenk. "Send your man down for it in the near future." He nodded at Jacob.

"We could make a car for it," said Maurice after Mr. Klenk had left.

"There's a busted baby carriage in front of my building," said Jacob.

"Bring the wheels," said Maurice.

Jacob began to put on all his outdoor clothes.

"I never heard of a bear having a car," he said.

"Why not?" asked Maurice.

THE DOG

Maurice and Jacob were unable to begin building a car for the bear the next day because Patsy arrived early in the morning.

Patsy was a large soft dog with beady eyes. She was wearing a plaid wool coat. Maurice and she stared at each other for several minutes. She was nearly as tall as he was. Then she walked straight into Maurice's room. When she came out a minute later, she had an oatmeal box in her mouth.

"Give me that!" demanded Maurice. Patsy lowered herself slowly on her four legs until she was lying on the floor with the box in her teeth.

Maurice looked at his mother. She was smiling and nodding. He looked at his father who was just about to leave for work.

"Nice dog," said his father.

"Give it back," whispered Maurice to Patsy. She stared at him. Then she turned her head suddenly, and Maurice snatched the oatmeal box and ran to his room with it. He closed the door and went back to the kitchen to finish his bacon and cocoa.

When he came out to put on his galoshes before going to school, Patsy was sitting in the living room. She was chewing an ear section of the witch doctor's mask. He ran to her and grabbed it. Patsy stood up and wagged her tail. Maurice could see she was just waiting for him to leave. He pretended to go to the front door, then suddenly turned and tiptoed back to his room. Patsy was already in it, sniffing up at the hamster.

"Please leave my room," said Maurice. Patsy looked at him over her back. He slipped his fingers beneath her collar and pulled. It was difficult to drag such a big dog. His mother came to the door. "Don't bully the dog," she said. "Good Patsy!"

"I don't want her in my room," said Maurice.

"She's so friendly," his mother said. Patsy wagged her tail and sat down on Maurice's foot.

"She was trying to eat the hamster," Maurice said.

"Oh!" exclaimed his mother. "You're exaggerating! She was only looking around. She probably misses your uncle."

Maurice looked at a round hole in his door near the knob where he and Jacob had dug out the lock and the latch months ago.

"Couldn't we put the lock back in?" he asked.

"Not now," said Mrs. Henry. "Now you go to school. You're going to be late!"

Right after his arithmetic class, Maurice asked the teacher for permission to go to the principal's office. The secretary said he could use the telephone for two minutes.

"Hello," said Maurice's mother.

"Is she in there?" asked Maurice.

"Who?" asked Mrs. Henry.

"Pull the octopus higher," said Maurice.

"Oh, Maurice," said Mrs. Henry, "as if I didn't have enough to do! Patsy doesn't want your octopus."

Maurice looked up at the clock.

"Can't you tie her to something?" Maurice asked.

"Stop fussing," said Mrs. Henry.

After school, Maurice ran all the way home. He was out of breath when he reached his front door.

Patsy was lying asleep in the living room. Maurice's things were all around her like a fortress. Her head was resting on the raccoon tail.

It took Maurice an hour to put everything back. Patsy watched him from the door.

"Thief!" he said to her. She wagged her tail.

The next day Maurice did not feel very well. His mother said he could stay home provided he kept to his bed. "None of this wandering around in bare feet," she said.

Maurice was happy to stay in his room. He watched Patsy as she paced back and forth outside his door. When she tried to sneak in, he shouted, "No, you don't!"

That afternoon he heard his mother speaking with his uncle on the telephone.

"Maurice and Patsy are inseparable," she said. "You were quite right. We must get him a dog of his own."

"A whole week," said Maurice to himself. He be-

gan to feel really sick. Suddenly Patsy made a dash for the chest of drawers. She put one paw on a drawer pull.

"Out!" shouted Maurice, standing up in the middle of his bed with the blankets flapping around him. Patsy ran from the room, but she sat down right in front of the door.

The next day Maurice felt poorly again. His mother took his temperature. He had no fever. His throat wasn't red. But his eyes looked strained. The strain came from staring through the dark at Patsy half the night. But the dog had fallen asleep before Maurice had and so she had been unable to steal a single thing from Maurice's room.

"I think you should go to school," said Mrs. Henry.

"No!" said Maurice, kneeling on his bed.

"Mercy! You don't have to kneel," she said. "What *is* the matter?"

"I can't go to school," Maurice said.

Mrs. Henry called Mr. Henry.

"I think he is developing a school phobia," Maurice heard her say to his father as they stood in the hall outside his room.

At that moment, Patsy raced in, threw herself at the bed, snatched a blanket, and made off with it. Maurice jumped to the floor and ran after her. They both slammed into Maurice's father.

"If you don't stop playing with Patsy, I'll have to send her home!" said Mr. Henry.

After that, it was easy. Maurice played with Patsy every minute he could, and soon his uncle came to get her. He dressed Patsy in her plaid coat, clipped on her leash, put on his hat, and left.

"You see?" said Maurice's father.

Maurice nodded.

5.   THE BEAR

One Saturday morning, a few weeks after Patsy had left, Maurice awoke at six o'clock. His window was blurred because it was raining so hard. The hamster stirred in its cage.

"You're up too early," Maurice said. The robin lifted one wing slowly and opened its good eye. Maurice went into the kitchen and made himself a grape-jelly sandwich. It felt good to be eating a sandwich and walking down the hall so early in the morning. No one else was awake. He gave a piece of bread crust to the robin and one to the hamster. Then he got dressed.

Soon there was a soft knock on the front door. It

was Jacob, who always arrived early on Saturday mornings and who usually brought something with him. Today he was carrying a paper sack.

"Do you want a jelly sandwich?" asked Maurice. Jacob nodded. Then he showed Maurice what he had brought in the bag.

"What is it?" asked Maurice.

"I think it's for weighing things. I found it in a box on the street," Jacob said, holding up a large white scale. The paint was chipped, and when Maurice pressed his hand down on the platform, the needle on the dial jiggled.

"Your arm weighs six pounds," said Jacob.

Maurice's mother walked by. She was yawning. She glanced into the room. "Good morning, children," she said.

"My arm is very heavy," said Maurice.

"That's nice," said Maurice's mother, and yawned again and walked on.

"I forgot to tell you," Jacob said. "Mr. Klenk said to come and get the bear."

Maurice put the scale on his bed. Then both boys ran to the front door and down the five flights of stairs to Mr. Klenk's room in the basement. Mr. Klenk was blowing on the cup of coffee he was holding in one hand. He still carried a broom in the other.

"It seems I hardly have time for coffee," said Mr. Klenk. "I'll be glad to get rid of that bear."

He left them standing at the door, peering into his room. There was so much cigar smoke in the air, it was hard to see the furniture. In a minute Mr. Klenk was back, pushing the bear before him. The bear's feet were strapped into roller skates. It was as tall as Jacob.

"Here he is," said Mr. Klenk. "Think you can handle him?"

Jacob and Maurice stared. The bear was plump. Its fur was black. Its two front paws stuck out straight in front of it. The claws were of different lengths, and some of them pointed upward as though the bear had been pushing against a wall.

"Why is it wearing skates?" asked Maurice.

"It came that way," said Mr. Klenk.

"It looks tired," said Jacob.

"It had a long sea voyage, all the way from South America."

Maurice pulled and Jacob pushed and they got the bear up the stairs all the way to Maurice's front door, and inside. Because of the skates the bear moved easily on a level surface, but it had been a slippery business getting it up the stairs.

"I think we'd better wait a while before we show it to my mother and father," said Maurice. "They don't like surprises."

"Mine neither," Jacob said.

Maurice said, "Why don't you get your hat and coat and put them on the bear and maybe they'll think it's you if we push him down the hall fast."

Jacob went to get his outdoor clothes. They dressed the bear, pulling Jacob's hat almost all the way down its muzzle. Then, running, they propelled it down the hall. As they went by his parents' bedroom, Maurice's father poked his head around the door.

"Who's that?" asked Mr. Henry in a sleepy voice.

"Jacob!" said Maurice.

"Maurice!" said Jacob.

Mr. Henry went back to bed. "You shouldn't roller-skate in the house," he said.

At last they got the bear into a corner of Maurice's room. "The bear has a funny smell," said Jacob.

"You're right," said Maurice. "But we'll have to get used to it. "

34

They took Jacob's clothes off the bear. Then they stood and looked at it. It was pleasant to have a big animal in the room with them, even if it was stuffed.

"Maurice," Mrs. Henry called. "Come and drink your apple juice."

"We'll have to disguise it. Then one day when they're feeling good I'll just tell them I have a bear," said Maurice in a whisper. Then he called out, "We'll be there in a minute."

"Couldn't we hide it under the bed for a while?" asked Jacob.

"No," said Maurice. "It won't fit because the Victrola's there. But wait a minute." Maurice opened his closet door and pulled out a heap of clothing. Pretty soon he found what he wanted. It was a penguin costume.

"It was for Halloween," said Maurice.

They started dressing the bear. They had to cut holes in the feet to fit the costume over the bear's roller skates. Then they zipped up the front and pushed the bear between the table and the window. Nothing was left showing of it except the big bumps where its paws were.

Then they went to the kitchen and had apple juice and doughnuts.

PATSY AGAIN

The next day, which was Sunday, Maurice's uncle was coming to visit. When Maurice heard that Patsy was coming with him, he went to his room and began to pile up things behind his door.

Maurice's father knocked, and Maurice opened the door a crack.

"Maurice," he said, "you'll have to clean out the hamster's cage. There's a very strong smell coming from your room."

"All right," said Maurice. "I'll do it right now."

He looked at the bear in its penguin costume.

"I wonder if I could spray you with perfume," he said.

Then he took a piece of rope and tied one end of it around the bear's neck and the other to his bed-

post. If somebody came in, he decided, he would just
roll the bear out the window and then pull it back
into the room when the coast was clear.

A few minutes later, he heard his mother let his
uncle in at the front door.

"Well, Lily, how are you?"

"Fine, and you?"

"Fine, and your husband?"

"Fine, and Patsy?"

"Fine."

"Fine," said Maurice to the hamster.

"And how is Maurice?" asked the uncle.

"Fine," said his mother.

"He'll be delighted to see Patsy."

"He surely will be delighted."

Maurice added his boots to the heap behind his door.

A large object suddenly hurtled down the hall and against Maurice's door. It was Patsy. The barricade gave way, and Patsy raced into the room, stomping and huffing and panting. The snake slid under its rock, the lizard froze, the hamster burrowed in its sawdust, and the bird closed its good eye.

Patsy stopped dead in her tracks. Maurice stood up slowly from where he had been crouching near his bed. Patsy's nose was in the air. She was sniffing. She slid one floppy paw forward, then another. Maurice sprang toward the bear, his arms outstretched.

"Don't lay a hand on that bear!" he cried.

It was too late. Patsy leaped. Over and down crashed the bear. All eight wheels of the roller skates spun in the air. Patsy sat on the bear and began to bay. Maurice could hear his mother, his father, and his uncle racing down the hall.

He ran to the window, flung it open, and deposited
the turtles on the floor. He grabbed a blanket from
his bed and threw it over Patsy, who fell into a tan-
gled heap alongside the bear. In a flash, Maurice had
the bear up on its skates and on the sill. He gave it
a shove, and out it went through the window, the
rope trailing behind it.

Mr. Klenk, who was sweeping the courtyard below and whistling softly to himself, heard the whir
of spinning roller skates and looked up.

"Ye gods!" he cried. "A giant penguin!"

"Today you are going to start your trumpet lessons," said Mrs. Henry. She held out a black case that reminded Maurice of a crocodile's head. Maurice put it on his bed and opened it. The trumpet glittered. He could see his face reflected in it.

He looked out of his window. A light rain was falling, a March rain that might be warm. It was exactly the kind of Saturday Maurice and Jacob liked to spend hunting for new things for the collection.

"You'll have to leave very soon," said Mrs. Henry as she started back to the kitchen to finish her cup of coffee. Maurice lifted the snake out of its cage. The snake wound itself around his wrist. It was a dull green color and quite small.

"The trouble with you is you don't have enough interests," he said to the snake. He put it back in its cage and pulled the chicken wire over the top. Then he put on his light jacket.

When he got to the front door, his mother said, "Just a minute. Haven't you forgotten something?" She was holding out the trumpet case. "And Maurice, really! It's raining! Put on your rubbers and your heavy jacket."

"Maurice, you must learn to be more responsible,"

said his father, who was standing at the other end of the hall eating a piece of whole-wheat toast.

Maurice went back to his room, dug into his closet, and found one of his rubbers and one of Jacob's. He wished he had been born wearing one pair of shoes and one suit of clothes.

Jacob was waiting for him in front of the building.

"Do your lessons really start today?" he asked.

"Yes," said Maurice. As he had guessed, it was a warm spring rain.

"Will you have to go every Saturday morning?"

"For six weeks," said Maurice. "Then they'll see."

"See what?" asked Jacob.

"If I get new interests."

On their way to the music school where Maurice was to take his lesson, they passed a big junk yard. A sign hung over the wire fence that surrounded the yard: *Auto Parts.* A man wearing a hat was walking around the piles of bumpers and tires and car bodies. Now and then he would kick an old fender.

"Why don't you wait for me in there," Maurice suggested. "Maybe you can find something good." The man with the hat walked into a little house not much bigger than a telephone booth. There was a small window in it. Maurice could see the man fiddling with a radio.

"Maybe he'll chase me away," said Jacob, looking at the man.

"I'll stay for a minute," said Maurice.

They walked toward the rear of the lot. The man looked out of his window but didn't seem to see them. He was chewing on a toothpick and still twisting the radio dials. Just behind the little house, Maurice and Jacob could see the long arm of a crane.

"Look at that!" said Maurice, pointing to a pyramid of heaped-up car parts. Poking out of the pile were hubcaps, fenders, tires, fan belts, radiator caps, pipes, window frames, steering wheels on shafts, and at the very top, lying on a car hood, a pair of headlights that looked almost new.

"We could use those headlights," said Maurice.

Jacob looked back at the little house. "He won't give them to us," he said.

"Maybe he'd make a trade," said Maurice.

"What could we trade?" asked Jacob.

"We'll think of something," Maurice answered. "But first we have to see those headlights."

"How will we get them?" asked Jacob.

"Climb," said Maurice. "See all the places you can put your feet?"

"Me?" asked Jacob.

"I think you can do it better. I'm heavier. If I tried it, everything might crash down," Maurice said.

"Are you going to ask him first if we can?" asked Jacob.

"He's not even looking at us," said Maurice.

Jacob put his right foot on a tire rim, then grabbed hold of the fender above him and brought his left foot up to another tire. Slowly he climbed toward the top, using the tires as steps.

Suddenly there was a loud clanging of metal, then bangs, screeches, and a crash. When the dust cleared, Maurice saw Jacob almost at the top of the pyramid, stretched out on a silver-colored car hood, clutching its sides.

The man ran out of his little house. When he saw Jacob, he threw his hat on the ground.

"What's the meaning of this!" he shouted.

"We'd like to make a trade," said Maurice.

"Trade! At a time like this?" bellowed the man. "Get off my property!"

"Help!" said Jacob in a weak voice.

"How will we get him down?" asked Maurice.

The man picked up his hat and jammed it back on his head. "Can't he fly?" he growled, then he turned and walked to the crane. He jumped up to the seat

and began to push the
levers around furiously.

"Don't worry," Maurice
called up to Jacob. "He's
going to get you down."

Jacob didn't answer. He
wasn't scared now, and
he rather liked being so
high above the ground.

There was a grinding of
gears and a maniacal

roar as the man maneuvered the crane into position.

"Clear away," shouted the man to Maurice. Maurice ran back toward the little house and watched as the claw at the end of the cables lowered its jaw, then clamped onto the hood where Jacob lay, gripped it, and lifted it down slowly like a plate. Several tires dislodged by the crane rolled along the ground.

"Well, get up," said Maurice to Jacob. Jacob was feeling sleepy. He shook himself a little and stood up.

"How was it?" asked Maurice.

"Okay," said Jacob.

The man jumped down from the crane, picked up a tire, and kicked it so hard it rolled all the way back to the pile. Then he started toward them.

Maurice and Jacob hurried to the gate. But Maurice stopped suddenly and darted into the little house, where he placed the trumpet on top of the radio.

"It's too late for my lesson anyhow," he said to Jacob as the man yelled after them,

"I've got a friend on the police force!"

On the way home, Jacob said, "What will your mother and father say?"

"Plenty!" said Maurice.

8. A BIRTHDAY PRESENT

In a few weeks Mr. and Mrs. Henry stopped mentioning the trumpet. After that, whenever Maurice happened to hear them, they were talking about moving to the country. "We'll have to move anyway, at the rate Maurice is going," Mrs. Henry said once. "If he puts one more thing in his room, he won't have a place to stand."

But Mr. Henry wanted to wait.

On a morning late in April, Mrs. Henry brought Maurice a glass of fresh orange juice on a little tray. There was a sign leaning against the glass. It read: "Happy Birthday to Maurice." She couldn't get into the room so Maurice got up from his bed and went to the door to get the tray.

Jacob came at noon and they had a birthday lunch. Maurice blew out all of his nine candles but he forgot to make a wish. Then Mr. and Mrs. Henry brought in a large box.

Maurice looked inside. It was a three-foot-long sailboat. The rigging was made of cord. The sails were of canvas, the winches really turned, and the hatches could be taken off and put back. It had two masts.

"It's a ketch," said Maurice's father, who was sitting on the floor next to him. "Look at those lines! Some boat!"

"Will it really sail?" asked Jacob.

"It will," said Mr. Henry.

"Can we take it to the lake right now?" asked Maurice.

"Yes," said Mr. Henry. "But be very, very careful with it."

Maurice's mother smiled. "It's nice to see you so interested in something," she said to Maurice.

The two boys carried the boat to the park. They dropped their jackets on the grass and sat down on the cement ledge that ran all around the lake. Then they rigged the sails.

A brisk wind was blowing. Maurice and Jacob slid

the boat into the water. Instantly, it raced toward the center of the lake, its sails puffed out with wind. The boys ran around to the other side, but Jacob suddenly stopped. His hair was blowing almost straight up.

"Come on!" shouted Maurice.

"Look!' said Jacob, pointing at the water. Two or three feet out from the shore, something glistened as the breeze lifted the water into small waves.

"Bedsprings," said Maurice.

"How can we get them?" asked Jacob.

Maurice sat down on the ground and took off his shoes and socks, but Jacob waded in after Maurice with his shoes on. The springs were heavy, and weeds were growing through them.

They dragged them onto the grass. Maurice put on his shoes and socks and jumped on the springs.

"We can borrow wire cutters from Mr. Klenk and make coils to put on our shoes."

"We can hook it up so it stretches across the room," said Jacob.

"I can pull it across the door so Patsy doesn't get through," said Maurice.

They picked up the springs and started home. Jacob's wet shoes squeaked.

Then Maurice stopped. "We forgot something," he said.

They dropped the springs and ran back to the lake. On the opposite side was the boat, its stern half-way up the cement ledge, its sails flapping.

"What are you going to tell them?" asked Jacob as they lifted the boat out of the water. The stern was smashed and the mainmast tilted.

"I don't know yet," answered Maurice.

"Could we say there was a little storm?"

"No, we'll have to tell them what really happened —that the boat went out of control," said Maurice.

"Because we weren't watching," said Jacob.

They put the boat on top of the springs; then with Maurice holding the front of the springs and Jacob the back, they started home.

At first, Maurice's father didn't say anything. Mrs. Henry told Jacob to go home and change his wet socks and shoes; then she went to the kitchen. Maurice heard her rattling pots and pans.

"If I had known you wanted bedsprings instead of a beautiful three-foot sailing ketch, I would have gotten you bedsprings," said Mr. Henry at last.

Maurice said nothing.

"Go to your room and think about what happened," said Mr. Henry.

Maurice put the sailboat under his bed next to the Victrola so he wouldn't have to look at it. He put a blanket on the bedsprings and sat down on them. One of the coils had come loose and was bobbing up beside him. He rested his arm on it.

He heard his parents talking the rest of the afternoon. His mother brought him a supper tray while it was still daylight.

Then Mr. Henry came and stood in Maurice's doorway. Maurice was still sitting on the springs.

"I have something to tell you," he said. "We have decided to move to the country as soon as school is over."

"How will I see Jacob?" asked Maurice.

"Jacob can take the bus. It's not very far. You can have a dog."

"Not Patsy!" asked Maurice.

"No," answered his father. "But your uncle has a racing bike he is going to give you. It's a little old, but it still goes."

"I'm sorry about the boat," said Maurice.

"Your mother and I are sorry too," said Mr. Henry. He came over and sat down next to Maurice on the bedsprings.

"They're still a little damp," he said.

Maurice gave him a corner of the blanket to sit on. They didn't speak about the sailboat. In fact, it was never mentioned again.

AN EXPLOSION

The Henrys moved to the country the day after school ended. Mrs. Henry said Maurice could take his collection if he could find something to pack it in. Mr. Klenk gave him an old steamer trunk with broken hinges. Jacob brought a length of rope to tie around it. Maurice was able to get everything into the trunk except the bedsprings. He gave them to Jacob.

The movers' truck drew up in front of Maurice's building around noon. Mr. Klenk, Jacob, and Maurice stood outside and watched the movers load the furniture on.

"I don't see how they can get all those things into the truck," said Jacob.

"They fit them together like a jigsaw puzzle," said Mr. Klenk.

The last items the movers brought down were Maurice's animals and his trunk. They placed the cages on the tops of bureaus at the front of the truck. They left the trunk at the back, near the tailgate.

"Can I ride in the truck with my things?" Maurice asked his father.

"If it's all right with the movers," said Mr. Henry.

Mr. Klenk waved his cigar at Maurice. "Come back and visit me," he said. "I'll keep an eye out for interesting things for your collection."

Jacob didn't say goodbye. He was coming out to visit the next day. He waved as Maurice hiked himself up onto the truck.

All the way through town, Maurice could see his mother and father driving behind in the rusty jeep they had bought for the country. But soon he lost sight of it as the truck pulled ahead.

Maurice walked to the front, winding through the furniture and crates, the boxes and baskets, to check up on his animals. The hamster was running on his wheel, but the robin, the snake, the lizard, and the salamanders were all asleep.

They turned off on a blacktop, then onto a dirt road. After that, the ride got bumpier. There were no buildings, no gasoline stations, no signs—only green hills and trees and birds sitting on telephone wires. Here and there a crumbling stone wall followed the curve of a hill. The sun was very warm, and the canvas curtains on either side of the truck's tailgate flapped back and forth.

All at once, there was a tremendous crash. The furniture rattled, the cages danced on top of the bureaus, the robin chirped, and the pots banged against each other. They had driven over a big bump. Maurice's trunk teetered as they rounded a curve, then flew out, hit a rock, and seemed to explode into the air. Maurice saw his collection flying in all directions, then drop out of sight down the hill.

The truck stopped just as the jeep arrived. Maurice's father came running up to Maurice and lifted him down. Then everyone went to look over the hill. Maurice's things lay scattered everywhere among the rocks and tall grass. Maurice sat down on the road.

Mrs. Henry knelt beside him.

56

"Wow!" said Maurice. "Did you see that?"

Mrs. Henry stood up.

"The whole trunk blew up!" said Maurice. "It flew out in the air and exploded!"

"You can start a new collection," said Mr. Henry.

But Maurice didn't hear him. He was thinking that even the paper sacks of water he and Jacob had once dropped from the roof to the courtyard hadn't made such a terrific noise. He had never seen anything like it.

Maurice's new room had one window and a slanted ceiling that was so low that Mr. and Mrs. Henry couldn't stand up straight beneath it.

When Maurice awoke the morning after the move, a branch was tapping against the windowpane and there were leaf-shaped shadows on the floor. Maurice wondered if he could step from the window to the big round branches of the tree that stood just outside. Just beyond the tree, Maurice could see a red barn. As he stared at it, a flock of birds flew from under the barn roof, circled in the sunlight, and flew back.

The room was empty except for Maurice's animals and his suitcase and the bed. The fields outside seemed empty too, except for the tall grass. The house was silent.

In the kitchen Maurice found a package of saltines and a glass of milk he had been too tired to finish the night before after all the unpacking.

Maurice's father walked in and sat down at the table. It was the same one that had been in Maurice's room in the city.

"Did you see the pump?" asked Mr. Henry.

"What's that?" asked Maurice.

"Sometimes there are storms, and the electricity goes off. Then you can use the hand pump to get water. It's just outside the door."

Maurice poked his finger into a little hole in the oilcloth.

"What do you think of the country?" asked Mr. Henry.

"It's okay," said Maurice.

"You are making a large hole in the oilcloth, Maurice. Why don't you take a look outside? Have you been to the barn?"

Maurice tried to balance four saltines against one other.

"Jacob will be here soon," said Mr. Henry. "You can take him to see the stream."

"What's in it?" asked Maurice.

"All right, Maurice," his father said, "you know what's in a stream!"

Maurice ate half a saltine. He wasn't very hungry.

"You'll get used to it here," said Mr. Henry. "It's new now. But you'll find lots of things to interest you."

At the word *things*, Maurice looked up at his father.

"There's nothing but grass," he said.

"Take a look in the barn," said Mr. Henry.

On his way out, Maurice tried the pump. He had to use both hands. Nothing happened for a moment; then a stream of cold bluish water gushed out on his feet. He squashed his way through the tall grass and the brambles to the barn.

The biggest door was padlocked, but next to it was a small door which hung half open from one hinge. He slipped inside.

He heard a great rustling of wings. For a moment

he stood still waiting for his eyes to get used to the dark. Then he looked straight up. The roof of the barn seemed miles above him. Small birds swooped through the rafters from which hung spider webs as big as trapeze nets. As soon as Maurice began to walk, an interesting musty smell arose from the floor. On his right were wooden stalls and on his left was an old hay wagon. One of its big wheels lay on the floor, half covered with hay. There were ladders of all sizes leaning up against the walls, and from the

posts that supported the overhead rafters hung an extraordinary assortment of objects.

"Fish nets," said Maurice aloud. "A hoe, a rake, a bucket, another bucket, a bamboo pole with a line and three fish hooks, a dog collar, mousetraps, a leather jacket, a pitchfork, a lantern." There were many other things made out of leather or wood or metal, but he didn't know what they were.

A big shaft of sunlight fell across the floor. Maurice turned and saw his father standing in the doorway. Bits of hay and dust floated around him.

"Your mother has gone to get Jacob at the bus stop," he said.

Maurice noticed several lengths of chain and a tire tube hanging from a nail near the door.

"Do you like the barn?" asked Mr. Henry.

"Yes," said Maurice.

"That's where they used to keep the hay," said Mr. Henry, pointing to a platform above the wagon. "But I don't think we're going to have cows or horses." Just then Jacob came to the door. He was carrying a paper bag.

"Come in and see my barn," said Maurice.

Jacob stepped inside.

"What's in the bag?" asked Maurice.

"Jelly doughnuts and a wrench Mr. Klenk gave me to give to you."

Maurice cleared the hay off the rim of the wagon wheel, and they sat down to eat their doughnuts.

"Your mother said there was a stream we could fish in," said Jacob.

"Not yet," said Maurice. "We have to fix up this barn. We have to find out what's in it. We can repair things. Like this wheel. We'll put it back on the wagon. Then, when we get too hot, we can go to the stream."

"What do we do first?" asked Jacob.

"First we have to find out the name of everything," said Maurice.

"Why?" asked Jacob.

"Because that's how you begin," answered Maurice. "Okay?"

"Okay," said Jacob.